SUPER FLY GUY

Tedd Arnold

Cartwheel
·B·O·O·K·S·®

SCHOLASTIC INC.
New York Toronto London Auckland Sydney
Mexico City New Delhi Hong Kong Buenos Aires

For Little Tate William
—T.A.

ISBN-13: 978-0-439-90374-5
ISBN-10: 0-439-90374-2

30 29 28   16 17/0

Printed in the U.S.A.   40
This edition first printing, May 2009

A boy had a pet fly.
The fly was named Fly Guy.
Fly Guy could say the boy's
name—

Chapter 1

One day Fly Guy went to school with Buzz.

Fly Guy learned about
reading and phonics.

He learned about art.

Then it was lunchtime.
Fly Guy loved the lunchroom.

He loved the dirty dishes.

He loved the smelly mop.

He loved the garbage cans.

Fly Guy met the lunch lady.
Her name was Roz.

"No flies in the
lunchroom!" Roz said.
Fly Guy said—

"This fly is smart," said Roz.
"He knows my name!"

ROZ

She fed Fly Guy chicken bones
and fish heads in sour milk.
Fly Guy was happy.

Chapter 2

Roz's boss was not happy.
"The children cannot eat
in a room full of flies!"
he said. "You are fired!"

Roz was sad. Fly Guy was sad.
Buzz and the children were sad
because Roz was a good cook.

The next day, Roz was gone.
Miss Muzzle was the new
lunch lady.

She made burnt peas and
turnips. No one in school
ate lunch—not even Fly Guy,
who ate almost anything.

Everyone missed Roz.
Even the boss missed Roz.

That night, Buzz made a plan.

Chapter 3

The next day, Fly Guy went to school again. In the lunchroom Fly Guy said—

Miss Muzzle looked up.
Fly Guy boinked her
on the nose.

BOINK

Miss Muzzle cried, "No flies in my lunchroom!"

She grabbed her swatter
and swung. She missed.

She missed again.

She missed again.

24

She missed again.

She missed again.

The boss was not happy.
"The children cannot eat
in this mess," he said.
"You are fired!"

The next day, Roz was back.
"You are a super Fly Guy!"

Roz made a special garbage soup for Super Fly Guy.

Fly Guy was happy.

Everyone was happy.